Mort the Sport

by **Robert Kraus**

illustrated by **John Himmelman**

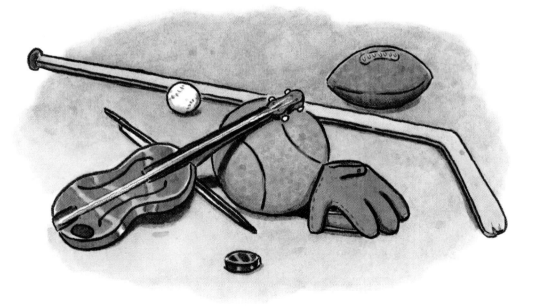

Orchard Books • New York

Orchard Books, A Grolier Company
95 Madison Avenue, New York, NY 10016

Manufactured in the United States of America
Printed and bound by Phoenix Color Corp.

The text of this book is set in 18 point Veljovic Medium.
The illustrations are watercolor.
Book design by Zara Design
1 3 5 7 9 10 8 6 4 2

Library of Congress Cataloging-in-Publication Data
Kraus, Robert, date.
Mort the sport / by Robert Kraus ; illustrated by John Himmelman.
p.   cm.
Summary: Mort's attempts to excel at playing both baseball and the violin make him so
confused that he decides to take up chess instead.
ISBN 0-531-30247-4 (trade : alk. paper).—ISBN 0-531-33247-0 (library : alk. paper)
[1. Baseball Fiction. 2. Violin Fiction. 3. Chess Fiction.]
I. Himmelman, John, ill. II. Title.
PZ7.K868Mn   2000   [Fic]—dc21   99-28574

For Pam, Parker, and Jack

—R.K.

*For Dad, who taught me how
to be a sport*

—J.H.

Mort was good at sports.

You name the sport, Mort was good at it:
basketball,

football,

soccer,

hockey,

and volleyball.

But Mort's best sport was baseball.
"Yea," Mort's dad cheered.
"Go for it, son!"

Mort's mother, though,
wanted him to play the violin.
"Music is so beautiful," she said.

To make his mother happy,
Mort took violin lessons
from Professor Manicotti.

Mort took his violin to ball games
so he could practice when he had the chance.

"Play ball!" yelled Mort's dad.
"Become a star."

"Practice makes perfect!" yelled Mort's mother.
Mort loved his mom and dad.
So Mort tried very hard to be *a sport.*

One day, though, the worst began to happen.
At practice, Mort swung his violin at the baseball.
Fortunately, he missed.

He was late for his violin lesson,
so he ran to Professor Manicotti's.
He took out his bat and began to play.

Mort ran back and forth,

back and forth, back and forth.

He got so mixed up
he couldn't play sports
or the violin.

"We're putting too much pressure
on Mort," said his mother.
Mort's father agreed.

"What do you want to play?"
they finally asked. "Baseball or the violin?"
"Chess," said Mort.
"I want to sit down."

**So Mort took up chess and became
Champion of the World.**